Sister Carrie

Sister Carrie

by

William H. Coles

Published November, 2016

Story in Literary Fiction
Salt Lake City, Utah 84101

www.storyinliteraryfiction.com
facebook.com/storyinliteraryfiction

Cover art and illustrations by David Riley

ISBN: 978-0-9984376-0-6 (softcover)
ISBN: 978-0-9984376-1-3 (hardcover)
ISBN: 978-0-9984376-2-0 (ebook)

CHAPTER 1

2003
Piedmont of North Carolina

Inside the cemetery—bordered by a waist-high iron fence, crowded with modest stone markers and wooden crosses, some draped with plastic flowers—two fresh graves waited side by side, flanked by the caskets of the mother and father of the Broward family. Carrie Broward, a tall, muscular girl with pretty facial features and short-cut straw-blond hair, stepped forward from the sparse crowd. Jessie Broward, her older sister, a full-figured woman with a close resemblance to her sister but with pecan-shell-brown hair, followed to lay flowers on their parents' caskets. The other Broward siblings, Henry and Martha, stood a few feet away, heads bowed and eyes closed.

At the cemetery's edge, a young Arab driver in a dark suit and tie leaned against one of the two freshly washed hearses, spotless but dull from decades of use. His eyes did not leave the sisters. A minister delivered a final prayer for the deceased. The gnarled fingers of an old woman sitting on a three-legged stool painfully searched the frets of her shabby guitar for the strummed chords of "Just a Closer Walk with Thee." The service concluded, the mourners drifted toward the church, and the undertaker directed workers to lift the straps of the first coffin for its descent into the earth.

The next morning, the four Broward children gathered to divide their parents' possessions at the modest, century-old family farmhouse with a tilted for-sale sign on a stick at the end of the dirt drive.

"I am not taking on responsibility for a seventeen-year-old," Henry said, pausing mid-brushstroke and turning from the window frame he was painting.

"Quiet, she'll hear you," Martha said from the kitchen, throwing a cracked and chipped casserole dish into a metal trash can with a crash of splintering glass, and turning back to scrub glassware in the sink.

Jessie went to the front door to look for Carrie. "She's carrying stuff out of the toolshed," she said.

"Don't let her throw out any power tools," Henry said.

"She's laying things out for us to see."

"She'll take the best."

"She doesn't want power tools."

"Anything of value."

"Stop it. You don't have an ounce of her goodness."

"You think so much of her. *You* take care of her."

"I've only got a one-bedroom apartment," Jessie said, picking up a broom and sweeping.

"Move out here with her," Martha said. "Take care of the place until we sell it."

"It's forty miles."

"Get a job closer."

"There's no jobs here. No people."

"We can't afford her living with us," Henry said. "Marie is trying to get into college."

Carrie came in the front door. Jessie stopped sweeping the fireplace hearth.

"Can I keep this?" Carrie asked, holding up a two-and-a-half-foot-high child's oak chair with a hoop back and spindle slats.

"It's junk," Henry said.

"It's was mother's when she was a little girl," Carrie said. "She told me."

"Bullshit."

"Leave it in the shed," Martha said. "Sell it with the house."

"I want it for my kids," Carrie said. She set the chair defiantly near the front door and went back to the shed to finish cleaning.

"That is exactly why I won't take her," Martha said. "Obstinate. Disrespectful. I have no responsibility to live with that for the rest of my life." A stemmed glass splintered as she threw it in the trash.

They worked in charged silence for a few minutes.

"You're the one, Jessie. You're closest to her," Henry said.

"She'd at least be able to stay close to where she was born," Martha added. "She doesn't have the smarts to make it in a big city."

"Move into a bigger apartment, for Christ's sake," Henry said to Jessie.

"And who will pay for that?" Jessie asked.

Silence.

"Well?"

Martha went somewhere into the back of the kitchen, out of view. Henry stared out the window and kept working.

"I'm not taking her on," Jessie said. "I can't afford it."

"Sell what's left after today," Martha said, coming back and wiping her hands on a dish towel.

"There's nothing of value," Jessie said. "You've taken everything."

"I'll try to send an allowance," Martha said.

"How much?"

"I can't afford more than a few dollars a month. Jake won't give anything extra to me. I'll have to take it out of my house budget."

"Then I get what's in the bank accounts," Jessie said.

"No way," Henry said. "I'm the executor."

"It's the only way I can take her on," Jessie said.

Martha picked up a box full of dishes and started toward her truck. She looked to Henry. "You've got more money than all of us put together," she said.

"I've got family responsibilities," Henry said.

"And a big boat," Martha retorted.

"I make just above poverty wage," Jessie said. "Hourly. Nothing guaranteed. No pension."

Martha reentered. "Give her the money, Henry. It can't be much anyway."

Henry paused. "Only part. And only if Carrie is living with her."

By late afternoon, cars and a van were packed, and Martha left for Michigan and Henry for Arizona. As Jessie locked up the house, she pretended not to see that Carrie had tucked the child's chair under some blankets in the back of her car.

Jessie loved Carrie as best she could—better than she did Martha and Henry, for that matter—and tried to convince herself she liked having Carrie around. What pissed her off was the family dumping Carrie on her. Henry and Martha still refused to consider taking Carrie in, even on a rotating schedule, and no money had been sent by either Henry or Martha. With her two rooms, a bathroom with only a shower, and a kitchenette, Carrie was never more than a few feet from her. And Carrie had no direction in life. She had dropped out of high school to work the farm, selling produce roadside and in town markets. She would never go back to school, and college had never been considered.

For weeks after the funeral, from her bedroom, Jessie heard Carrie's quiet sobs coming from the living room, where Carrie slept on the sofa bed. During the day Carrie had nothing to do, so Jessie got her a job in a movie theater working at the concession stand. It worked out pretty well. Carrie liked helping the patrons and considered her job a career to conquer. And she started staying more busy at home. Now when Jessie returned from her work as an assistant for an optometrist, she'd find Carrie polishing the family silver, scrubbing sinks and toilets, or vacuum cleaning the apartment. For recreation Carrie chatted on the Internet on Jessie's computer, or watched movies or late-night reruns of *I Love Lucy* on TV.

As Carrie settled in, Jessie's dream of a loving husband and a happy brood of her own children faded. Prayer brought no solution; Carrie would never go away. Jessie had no choice and she resolved to bring up Carrie with their parents' Christian principles, keep her innocent, and protect her from worldly sins.

CHAPTER 2

One Tuesday, almost four months after the funeral, Jessie waited at the apartment front door to take Carrie to work at the Movieplex. Carrie, who was in Jessie's cramped bedroom with the door open, typed laboriously on Jessie's computer with her index fingers. Mom's rocking chair—the aged, scratched, and dented oak gleaming now from oiling and polishing by Carrie—sat against the wall squeezed between the bed and the computer stand.

"Hurry, it's raining," Jessie called.

"I can take the bus," Carrie called back.

"I can't be late. Shut it off."

"He wants to meet me!" Carrie exclaimed as the screen displayed a chat-room return.

"Who?"

"Zamel."

"Zamel? What's with Zamel?"

"He says he saw me at the funeral."

Jessie entered the room. "You don't know him."

"He's single. He lives alone. He fixes computers and works part time for the funeral home."

"Turn it off. You can't tell crap on the Internet. He might be a rapist, or a serial killer."

"He's not."

"A terrorist, even!"

"He loves animals. He wants a puppy. He misses his mother in Iran."

"Don't promise him anything."

"He wants to meet me at the mall."

"No!"

"He wants to meet you, too."

"That will never happen."

Carrie typed a reply and turned off the computer.

"You didn't say yes, did you?" Jessie asked.

"I can do what I want."

"Not until you're eighteen. And maybe not then."

Carrie grabbed a jacket from the bed as Jessie slipped into her rain gear and opened the door.

"You are not going to see that boy!" Jessie said as they walked to the car.

Two days later, Jessie and Carrie sat at a white-painted metal table for four in the second-floor mall food court. Jessie wore jeans and a sweatshirt; Carrie had on tight slacks and a lace-trimmed blouse low cut to show cleavage, and orange plastic hoop earrings dangling from her ears.

"I hope he's not late," Carrie said for the second time.

"We're twenty minutes early," Jessie replied with irritation. She had no idea how to handle this infatuation that seemed to make Carrie contrary to everything she said. She picked up a picture of the guy that Carrie had printed from the Net. "I can't see his face," she said. It was fuzzy like a picture from a store surveillance camera.

Carrie jumped up. "There he is!"

Zamel rose inch by inch above the meshing top stair of the escalator. He was six inches shorter than Carrie and built like he was prepubescent, but he wore adult clothes—a black short-sleeved shirt, tan Sansabelt slacks, and white running shoes. His black hair shined, his white teeth gleamed when he smiled, contrasting with his dark skin. Carrie ran and took his hand but he glanced at Jessie and then, gently and shyly, pulled his hand away. Jessie wasn't ready to acknowledge him yet and remained impassive; still, he nodded to her as he and Carrie approached.

Zamel pulled out a chair for Carrie and then stood before Jessie, who was almost at eye level with him while sitting, and staring at him relentlessly.

"It is a pleasure to meet you," Zamel said.

"Really?"

"Carrie has told me all about you. You are like a mother to her."

"I'm her sister. She lives with me."

"She told me. I'm so sorry to hear about your dear parents. So sudden."

Jessie shook her head in disbelief. "You might as well sit down."

"It would be my pleasure to buy you a drink. I know Carrie loves Dr. Pepper with lots of ice."

Jessie paused, concerned that she was not Christian enough to be ashamed of her impulse to order something expensive. "Chocolate milkshake," she said.

"My favorite also." Zamel left for drinks.

Carrie beamed. "Isn't he wonderful? So polite."

"He's darker than I thought."

"He's Persian."

"Like Persia is in Africa somewhere. He's not one of us."

Carrie turned her head away in anger.

"Break it off now," Jessie said. "Don't let it get complicated."

"Be nice to him, Jessie. For me."

Jessie begrudgingly admired the way Zamel laid a brown paper napkin on the table, placed the milkshake on the napkin, removed the tops of the paper wrappers from two straws—careful to never touch them directly—and handed them to her, then presented another folded napkin before he served Carrie her Dr. Pepper. He had a cup of water without ice for himself.

"Thanks," Jessie said to Zamel, glancing sternly at Carrie to convince her she wasn't satisfied in any way by the performance.

"Pleased to have the opportunity," Zamel said.

"Are you legal?" Jessie asked.

"I have a student visa. I take classes at Stringer Community College. I hope to apply for a green card."

"You have family?"

"Yes. In Iran."

"You saw Carrie at the funeral?"

"I was there. Yes."

"You tracked her down?"

"Not exactly. I found her on the Internet. I work with computers." Jessie squinted, her brow creased.

Carrie clasped Zamel's arm. "Leave us, Jessie," she pleaded.

"I don't think so."

"You promised."

"I never . . ."

"P-l-e-a-s-e!"

Carrie and Zamel wore identical forlorn looks that made Jessie suspicious of predesigned agendas. She sighed inwardly and walked toward the Sears store entrance, looking back over her shoulder at the two of them, now talking intently.

Two hours later Jessie led Carrie by the arm from the mall to her Ford Focus. Zamel waited near the doors of the mall exit, grinning. *Exactly what had gone on?*

"He's so cool," Carrie said.

They walked to opposite sides of the car. Jessie paused before unlocking the doors.

"That's it. No more, Carrie. He's not right for you."

Carrie tensed. They got in the car. Jessie put the key in the ignition. "We're going to the museum next Sunday," Carrie said.

In the name of God! She's out of control, Jessie thought. This had to be the end, not the beginning. *I'm not letting my sister fall for some Internet guy.* She cringed inwardly at Carrie's blatant disregard for her authority.

"Absolutely not!" Jessie said. "Tell him no."

"I can go by bus. He doesn't have a car."

Jessie started the engine. "It's over. I mean it." She backed out of the parking space. Carrie stared determinedly out the side window, straining for a last glimpse of Zamel.

CHAPTER 3

S unday was a free day at the museum. Jessie waited with Carrie outside the front door. Zamel walked briskly from the bus stop carrying a bunch of flowers, the stems wrapped in a paper towel: daisies, bluebonnets, Queen Anne's lace, a few dandelions, a white blossom, a few pussy willows. *He probably found them in a field.*

He bowed to a smiling Carrie, then presented the flowers to Jessie. They had clearly cooked this up in their Internet chats. Jessie's eyes moistened but she quickly recovered with a stern look, struggling to hide pleasure that was impossible to explain and out of proportion to the gift of the scraggly bouquet.

"Do you like them?" Zamel asked.

"They're all right," Jessie said.

"For a beautiful lady."

"Monkey babble." Jessie pulled her keys from her jacket pocket. "Wait here," she said, taking the bouquet and walking to her parked car.

She opened the trunk and carefully positioned the flowers. She freed a bloom in danger of being crushed by the closing lid. She twisted a stem to free a bluebell. She locked the car and smiled reluctantly to herself, making sure Zamel and Carrie could not see her pleasure.

Jessie followed Carrie and Zamel through the turnstiles into the lobby. Zamel picked up a guide map at an information kiosk and traced a route through the galleries with his finger. As he and Carrie set off, Jessie followed yards behind, keeping them in sight, up the grand staircase to the galleries.

Jessie browsed alone in the main gallery, careful to position herself so she didn't lose sight of Carrie and Zamel, side by side, in an adjacent gallery. A Victorian reproduction of a life-size bronze statue of a nude male Greek—in full extension throwing a discus—caught her eye. The genitalia were worn shiny smooth from the touches of art patrons. After a quick feel, Jessie pulled back her hand and furtively glanced over to see if Carrie and Zamel had seen. *I can't believe I did that!* Carrie and Zamel we're staring intently at a painting the size of a barn door of a blue eyeball on a yellow background. When they turned, Jessie looked to a marble Madonna-and-infant statue. When she looked again to Carrie and Zamel, she blushed with humiliation. *They saw me.* They were laughing.

Flustered, she moved along quickly, unable to concentrate on the art. Carrie and Zamel had disappeared.

She paused to calm down and collect her thoughts. She had every right to touch that statue. It's not like a sin. Thousands of others had done it. And she was here to protect Carrie. Don't get distracted! When she saw Carrie and Zamel cross a corridor a few minutes later, she headed toward them; Zamel left Carrie when he saw Jessie coming.

"What's wrong with him?" she asked Carrie.

"He wants to be alone with me and he's afraid to hurt your feelings."

But Jessie wondered if he might have been offended by the touch. Something in his religion maybe. *He's no doubt sexist!* She took Carrie's arm. "This isn't working."

"It's wonderful." Carrie pulled away.

Jessie grabbed Carrie's arm. "Let's go."

Zamel arrived. "It is wonderful painting, don't you think?" he said, pointing vaguely to a wall covered with paintings. "Maybe you join us later for a look at the mummy?"

"What mummy?"

"I think in the Egyptian display in the basement."

Jessie shook her head in disbelief. "You're too smooth for your own good."

"I mean no offense, Miss Jessie."

"You can't offend me. I don't listen."

"I just meant . . ."

"Please, Jessie, just for a little while," Carrie said again.

"Where will you go?"

"Just around here."

"Maybe in sculpture?" Zamel said.

"Don't leave modern art," Jessie said, thinking specifically about the nudes in sculpture. With just paintings on the wall and only one skinny stick-sculpture of a saint in the gallery center there was little to hide behind in modern art, and little to identify in the abstract imagery that might be erotic to the young.

"As you wish," Zamel said to Jessie.

"I'll be around. You just won't see me."

CHAPTER 4

An hour later, Jessie sat alone at a small table for two in the museum cafeteria. Two plates of mostly eaten pastries were on a brown plastic tray with a half-full cup of mocha coffee and an empty Diet Sprite bottle. Jessie stared without focus, her lips tight with frustration.

There were many people and few seats. A man grabbed the back of the other chair at her table. He was only a few years older than her twenty-five, balding, with a stubble of beard growth and a full mustache. Tinted glasses shrouded his eyes. His hands were strong, with sure movements.

"Can I sit here?" he asked.

She shrugged without looking at him. "There are other tables."

"Why not here?"

She saw his determination, deliberately surveying him.

"Suit yourself."

He sat. "Harold Lester," he said. He held out his hand.

She waved him off. "I'm not in the mood."

"I know you from church."

"I've never seen you."

"No. When we were in high school."

"I went to church on Easter and Christmas in those days." She stared for a few seconds. "I don't remember you."

"I looked different then," he said.

"I would hope so."

Next to them a family settled in at a table the mother had been saving; the parents yelled at the boisterous children to be quiet. Harold sipped his coffee.

"You still live on the farm?" Harold asked.

"I'm from the planet Elagron, in the nebular galaxy," Jessie said.

"An alien who likes art? Don't find many of those."

"I'm chaperoning my sister," she said testily.

"The mean one?"

"Not Martha. The young one."

"In the cafeteria?"

"She's in modern art."

"She's a cube?"

Jessie looked away, irritated by her urge to smile.

They avoided each other's gazes and sank into silence while the family next to them argued loudly. Harold got up—to leave, she thought. She suddenly didn't want to be alone. He was lost in the crowd near the café. *There he is. Good.* He returned with more coffee for him and a chocolate chip cookie wrapped in cellophane for her that he set on her tray.

Jessie placed the cookie on the table and shoved it toward him. "I don't want that." She was irritated that she wanted him to stay. She didn't trust him, but he seemed interested in her.

Harold sat. "You going to stay here all day?" he asked.

"Look. My sister's in love with this guy who's trying to put the make on her at this very moment. I don't plan to let anything happen. I mean *anything!*"

"She still underage?"

"She's almost seventeen. But she's my little sister."

"Let nature do its thing."

"She met the guy online. He's foreign. He's small, and dark. And he's a bozo."

"I've got a sister. She married a black guy—like from Africa. Two happy peas in a pod."

"That's different."

Harold had no response for a few seconds. "Relax," he said. "Not much can happen in a crowded art gallery."

"You don't know that. They're cooking up something right now. I guarantee it."

"And you left them alone?"

"What do you care?" Now she felt guilty. "It doesn't make me feel better, your saying that."

A wall clock showed five to four. She stood and shouldered her bag. "Time to go."

Harold stacked trash on the tray without standing. "Leave mine," Jessie said. "They pick up."

Harold cleared the table anyway. "Enjoyed talking to you," he said.

Jessie walked off. She still didn't remember him from high school. Probably he lied, or had been so nerdy no one remembered him. He had a used-too-many-times look that meant he didn't think enough of himself to try to be attractive or memorable. Besides, the one she really cared for was an attractive, successful, strong-willed man who had thrilled—well, at least he seemed to care—her once or twice a week for more than a year now. He was her boss, and he was married, but he wanted her, which made her like her image in the bathroom mirror, and helped her not think about adultery, which she'd come to believe could not exist where true love dwelled.

She looked back, but Harold Lester wasn't following.

CHAPTER 5

In minutes Jessie was in the modern gallery. Carrie and Zamel held hands, standing in front of an unframed all-black rectangular painting. As Jessie approached, Carrie left him to face Jessie alone. Zamel stayed within easy hearing distance.

"Zamel wants to get married," Carrie said.

Jessie gasped. "You've only had one date."

"We talk all the time on the Net. He knows of a garage apartment next to his cousin and her husband in Butner. There's a bus. I could keep my job. Clean your place once a week."

Zamel closed in. "Miss Jessie. I must express my interest in Miss Carrie."

He had a dreamy, if not a little forlorn, look. "Go away," Jessie said.

She fought the idea that he might be sincere.

"Maybe you would like to talk woman to woman for a while?" Zamel asked.

I've got to get rid of this jerk. It was time to set things straight. "Stay here," she said to Carrie. She grabbed Zamel by the arm, overcame his resistance, and forced him to walk beside her into the next gallery behind a sarcophagus—out of view of Carrie. Zamel tilted his head back to look up to her.

"Stay away from my sister," Jessie said.

"I will not do that. She is object of my affections."

"She is a child."

"She is a woman to make any man good wife."

"She's never been with a man. She doesn't know . . ."

"She has told me many times she is chaste."

"Chaste?"

"I too have withheld relations."

Jessie was at a loss for words for many seconds. "Look. We are leaving. Don't follow. And never speak to my sister again."

"I cannot do that."

"You've got no choice."

Jessie found Carrie staring at a Renaissance painting of a half-nude Venus embraced by Mars. Venus's eyes were focused to infinity, as if she were angrily dissecting a distant galaxy. "Let's go," Jessie said.

"No, Jessie."

"It's sex. He wants your sex!"

Jessie dragged a defiant Carrie by the arm into another room farther away from Zamel. Carrie twisted away. Zamel approached.

"He's an alien," Jessie said in a low voice to Carrie's ear. "He's American," Carrie replied.

"He is not American! You are his green-card solution. Did you think of that?"

Carrie looked puzzled, not knowing what a green card was.

Zamel approached and stepped in front of Jessie. "She is not my green card solution!"

"Do you have one?"

"I will apply."

"There! An American wife might help! Deny that! And what will you do?"

"I go to school. I'll switch to Piedmont Community College for my degree."

"He's had almost a year of college," Carrie said defensively.

Jessie's clenched hands gripped the sides of her skirt. "There is nothing on God's green earth that will ever make you acceptable. Nothing!" she said to Zamel.

Carrie straightened. "Stop, Jessie." Carrie paused. Took a deep breath. "I've told him yes."

Zamel moved to close the gap between him and Carrie and took her hand. "I am very happy," he said.

"I'm going to unplug the computer," Jessie said.

"I want a family," Carrie said.

"You're not married yet!"

Zamel's smile had not changed. "We will have a wonderful family."

Jessie shoved Zamel back and pulled Carrie out of earshot. "I will never, never allow you to marry this Zamel whatever-his-name-is. Never!"

Carrie ran to Zamel, who stood now in the open arch between the galleries. She kissed him on the cheek. "She's silly sometimes. She'll be all right. I know her. She barks but never bites."

Jessie reached them quickly. She grabbed Carrie's arm, dragging her toward the exit. Zamel followed at a distance.

"It's over!" Jessie announced. She forced Carrie out of the museum double doors, between parked cars. Zamel watched from the building's exit, his face dark with concern.

CHAPTER 6

The Reverend Luther Coffey opened the door to his office in the administrative/recreational wing, just behind the twin-steeple red-brick Baptist church. Jessie and Carrie entered. He directed them to upholstered chairs in front of his polished mahogany desk.

The Reverend, at thirty-five, envied the youth of Carrie and Jessie. He wore his white clergy collar like a Catholic priest. He had brushed his short-cut hair two separate times before they entered. He wore glasses with thin gold-wire frames to project authority—authority he did not feel here with the sisters, who aroused him in ways he could not suppress and feared to be sinful.

"Jessie! Rarely I see you these days." He lowered himself into his leather swivel chair as if sitting on a throne. Through his apprehension of being insignificant, he forced a smile, his lips together.

Jessie made no attempt to greet him. "I brought Carrie to talk to you."

He looked to Carrie. "Jessie told me you want to marry."

"Yes, sir," Carrie said.

"I've told her it's wrong from the beginning," Jessie said.

"Have you known him long?" the Reverend asked Carrie, although he knew it had only been weeks.

Jessie answered. "They've had two dates."

"Don't start . . ." Carrie began.

"It's the truth, isn't it? Or have you been sneaking around that I don't know about?"

Carrie looked down, too angry for words.

Jessie shook her head. "I've tried. God, how I've tried."

The Reverend spoke up. "Let her speak for herself, Jessie."

Carrie leaned forward intently. "Will you marry us?"

He already had his answer ready. "It's too early to think about that. You and your friend—are you engaged?"

"Yes, sir."

"She doesn't have a ring," Jessie said.

"I don't need a ring," Carrie said. "Do I?" she asked the Reverend.

"A ring is a symbol of deep commitment," the Reverend said.

"He doesn't have the money now," Carrie said. "He promised he'll have it later."

"See! He doesn't have commitment," Jessie said.

"That's a lie," Carrie retorted.

"Rings cost money," Jessie said. "Where would that jerk get the money?"

"A ring doesn't have to be expensive," Carrie said.

"There's more to it than that," the Reverend said. He started on the plan he'd outlined before they arrived. "You could come for sessions with this boy. There are things to be explored, decisions to be made. Then you could start planning for the future together."

"He'll never come for sessions," Jessie said emphatically.

"You don't know what he'll do," Carrie said.

"Is he of the faith?" the Reverend asked. Jessie's concern impressed him. She had taken over the motherly role for Carrie quickly and efficiently. He admired that. Liked her for it.

"No, sir," Carrie said.

"He's Muslim," Jessie said. "Not even Christian."

The Reverend addressed Carrie. "Do you think he can be saved? Could you help him convert?"

Carrie avoided his gaze.

"Ask him, my child," the Reverend said to Carrie. "He might be the major convert of the season."

"I don't see baptism for this guy, now or ever," Jessie said. "His name's Zamel. Does that sound like a Christ disciple?"

The Reverend ignored Jessie, then spoke to Carrie. "I could talk to him. Man to man. Ask things your father might have asked. Bring up the possibility of conversion."

"He'll meet with you. He said he would," Carrie said.

Jessie glared at Carrie. "He'll never show."

"He's not like that," Carrie said.

"Let's give him chance, Jessie," the Reverend said. He looked at Carrie. "Wednesday afternoon at two?"

"He works."

"Thursday evening, then. At seven?"

Jessie looked dubious. "You want them both?"

He hadn't considered including Carrie, or Jessie. It was not a good idea. "Maybe Zamel alone," he said. "Then you later," he added, looking at Carrie.

Jessie drove intently, staring ahead. Carrie looked out the side window. "The Reverend will never marry you to someone outside the faith. It would be his sin—and yours," Jessie said.

Carrie stayed silent until they were almost home. "I'm not going to change my mind."

Jessie winced at her growing loss of what control she had had over Carrie. Carrie had lost her indecisive, ever-present innocence to all things serious; she was snarled in love. It was as if she were adopted or something. And not at all like the sisters they had been before their parents died. Jessie appealed for help. "Pray," she said to Carrie, "Ask

God for wisdom and guidance."

Carrie's face tightened and she looked away.

Jessie angered. "I'm speaking to you!"

Carrie still said nothing, even in the minutes it took for Jessie to nose into a parking space at the apartment complex.

CHAPTER 7

Jessie entered the Reverend's church consultation office with Zamel, her hand gripping his upper arm as if he were an errant child. The Reverend stayed behind his desk and did not stand.

"This is the guy," Jessie said.

"I am Zamel." Zamel reached awkwardly across the desk to shake the Reverend's hand.

"Welcome," the Reverend said.

"It is my honor, sir."

"Sit down." Jessie sat, too.

"I thought he was to come alone?" the Reverend asked Jessie.

"I wanted to come alone," Zamel said.

"There you go," Jessie said. "No respect."

"It's what we agreed," the Reverend said to Jessie.

"I thought it best," Jessie said defensively, offended at the Reverend's rebuke.

The Reverend ignored Jessie's hostility. "You would like to marry our Carrie?" he asked Zamel.

"We are very compatible."

"You are not Christian?"

"No sir, I am not. But I have many family and friends who have married Christians. Our religions are highly compatible."

The Reverend frowned. "You speak like an intelligent man. How can you believe mixing religions can be good?"

"We are in love, sir."

Jessie spoke to both Zamel and the Reverend. "Carrie doesn't know what love is."

"I beg to differ, Miss Jessie. She is not a child," Zamel said.

"But she is Christian. I think that is Jessie's point," the Reverend said.

"She is acceptable to me," Zamel countered.

"We would welcome you in the church," the Reverend said.

"I would be pleased to consider it," Zamel said.

"Before you get married?" Jessie asked.

"Yes, ma'am. If it's possible."

"You would need to attend our classes for converts," the Reverend said. "They're excellent."

"It's not a one-shot deal," Jessie said to Zamel. "It takes time."

"Of course I will give it consideration," Zamel said. "I will always do what is best for my Carrie."

The Reverend reached into a drawer for an appointment book and then extended a printed sheet of paper to Zamel. "Wednesday nights. Seven to ten. I can have you in the class next week."

Zamel took the paper and read.

The Reverend continued. "You can sign at the bottom. The tuition is payable in installments. Twenty dollars for the registration fee up front."

Zamel took the paper and picked up the pen that the Reverend had pushed toward him on the desk. But he did not sign. "I must wait for my payday."

"The fee is required," said the Reverend.

"Yes, sir. Of course."

The Reverend considered. "Your payday will be fine," he said, "You can sign up then, but you'll have to pay the initial installment and the registration fee, too, before starting."

Zamel returned the pen and stood. "Is that all, sir?"

Jessie spoke to Zamel. "Go to the car. I want to talk to the Reverend."

When the door closed, Jessie took a seat again. The Reverend came from behind the desk, pulled a chair close to Jessie, and sat.

"I never knew you charged for conversion classes," Jessie said.

The Reverend smiled. "We never charge. But I thought I'd test his commitment."

"He'll never pay."

"I won't marry them unless he's Christian. He's a polite young man, but I find mixed marriages appallingly unsuccessful. And I've always liked Carrie. I want to discourage him."

"You promise? You'll never marry them, Christian or not?" Jessie said.

"Trust me. He'll never convert." The Reverend smiled.

They both stood. The Reverend took Jessie's hand in both of his. Jessie flinched almost imperceptibly at the intimacy of the gesture.

"Thank you for coming," the Reverend said with excessive intensity. "I'll pray for Carrie. You should, too."

The Reverend still held Jessie's hand in his sweaty grasp. *God, he's creepy sometimes.* She pulled her hand away quickly, then headed for the door.

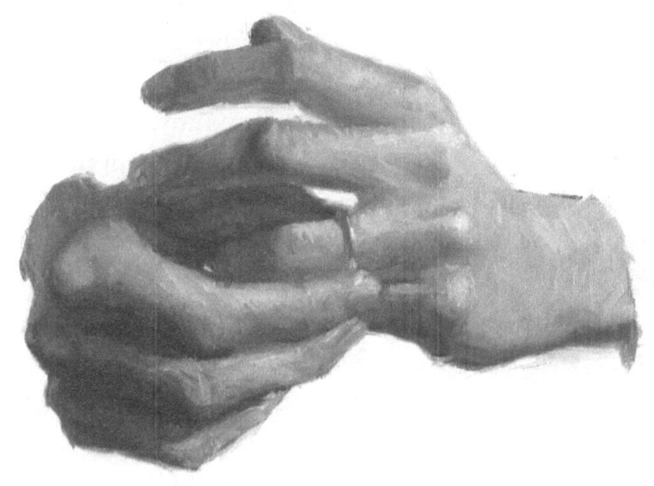

CHAPTER 8

Two weeks later, Jessie returned to the apartment early after work, worried about Carrie and her plans. A waist-high, taped and sealed packing box half-blocked the door. Carrie was packing an open suitcase on her sofa bed. Jessie walked straight to Carrie. A silver wedding band glinted on Carrie's finger in the afternoon light from the bedroom window. Jessie froze, waiting for an explanation. "Talk to me!" she finally said.

Carrie kept packing, refusing to look.

"After all I've done for you. The sacrifices. The worry." Jessie swore. "What about Mom and Dad? They wouldn't approve. They'd hate him."

Carrie paused. Her jaw clenched.

"In God's name, you owe it to their memory," Jessie insisted.

"Shut up!" Carrie cried.

"Just wearing a ring doesn't make you married, you know. You've got to have a church wedding with a real minister."

Carrie closed the top of the suitcase and faced Jessie. "It's all legal.

It's Muslim."

"My God. You've always dreamed of a church wedding."

"Zamel loves me. You'll never have that with Patrick."

"I don't want a foreigner for a brother-in-law," Jessie said, her emotions out of control.

After a few seconds, Carrie smiled hesitantly, searching Jessie's face for a sign of pleasure. Would Jessie ever accept her happiness with Zamel?

Jessie refused to respond. She sobbed. Carrie went back to packing.

"I hope you'll be happy," Jessie finally managed, but she couldn't hide the sarcasm in her voice.

A rusted pickup truck driven by a male Arab pulled into a parking space in front of the apartment. Zamel got out of the passenger side and walked slowly to Carrie; she hugged him. He reacted hesitantly at first, then embraced her. He walked over to Jessie and took both her hands in his. She reluctantly allowed him to come face to face with her.

"I am indeed fortunate to have such a beautiful sister of you," he said.

How irritating, this happiness on his face. "That's garbage," she said. "You know it. Besides, I'll never be your sister."

"She's a sister-in-law, Zamel," Carrie said.

"I know!" Zamel said brusquely. He carried out the smaller box and Carrie followed with the suitcase. They returned for the big box and positioned themselves one on each side. Jessie made no move to help.

"You'll come visit?" Carrie asked Jessie.

"I don't think so."

Carrie looked away. She still wanted Jessie's blessing.

Zamel tugged the box and with his eyes directed Carrie to help. "You are always welcome at our place," he said to Jessie. "You are family," he said over his shoulder. They joggled the box through the door and carried it down the walk.

Jessie followed them out the door but stopped at the top of the steps. She refused to expose how empty she felt. How abandoned. She went back inside before they were even near the truck. She closed the door, leaned against the wall, and cried.

CHAPTER 9

Zamel's place was a rented two-car garage with no conversions for comfort—no interior walls, and light from the outside seeping in only through a small rectangular glass window on a side door and the single long slits of frosted glass on each of the two sliding front doors. A sink, a knee-high refrigerator on the floor, and a four-burner stove clustered in the rear corner. The only furniture in the room was an aluminum-tube folding chair with plastic woven strips on the back and seat, and a small wooden table. A TV set sat on the floor near the single electrical outlet, and a box-spring mattress on a metal frame was to the side. Indelible oil stains from years of leaky engines stained the bare concrete floor. There was a toilet and a shower that was a showerhead attached to a garden hose, tied loosely to metal tracks that supported the retractable garage doors. Shower water drained over the sloping floor to a central rusty drain.

On their wedding night, Carrie made a cheese and mayonnaise sandwich for each of them. She lit a candle, melted the bottom end, placed it in a saucer, and set it on a packing box. They sat on the floor near the stove, holding their plates. After dinner, she expertly tucked stained white sheets onto the mattress. It was twilight. She washed the plates in the sink and dried them with a clean but ragged towel and stacked them below the sink where the pipes were. Without a word she took off her T-shirt, folded it, and put it on her closed suitcase. She placed her bra on top of the shirt. She slipped out of her untied pink sneakers, unbuttoned the top of her jeans, and undressed with a reticent lack of haste, worried at her lack of knowing how to please.

"We must bathe," Zamel said, reaching into a Walmart bag and handing her a just-bought-today towel. "You go first."

A toilet near the front corner of the garage was set directly on the cement. Behind it, she twisted the faucet handle on a T-valve to start the flow of water into the hose that led to the showerhead. After a few seconds, water splashed on her shoulders. She showered and dried, and walked to the bed. Zamel was undressed. He covered his manhood with a wadded shirt.

Carrie sat on the edge of the bed as Zamel showered, her arms wrapped around her knees, the towel around her shoulders. She watched Zamel dry, and held her breath as he walked to her with the towel in his hand. He turned off the bare lightbulb dangling from the ceiling over the sink. A cloudless sky filtered weak rays of dim light through the narrow rectangular frosted windows on the garage doors.

"Zamel," she said softly.

He positioned her over the bed, her knees on the floor, her elbows on a pillow on the mattress, her face inches from the sheets, and he took her standing up. She gave a painful gasp. He was finished in seconds. When she realized he was complete, she fell forward on the bed and rolled over.

"Hold me, Zamel," she said.

His face was a shadow. "I could not contain it," he said. He sat on the bed and put his head in his hands.

"I love you," she said.

He moved rapidly into the shadows on the other side of the garage. It was dark now, the night light from outside providing barely enough illumination to maneuver.

Carrie lay on her back with a blanket over her. She heard Zamel's breathing, but could only see his blurred silhouette in the chair.

"Zamel," she said softly. She waited. "That was very good."

She held her breath in the silence.

He spoke, and she started breathing again. "You make me happy," he said. "You are a very good wife."

Carrie ignored the rodent scurrying outside the wall near the head of the bed. She was too happy to care, and enjoyed her pleasure before falling asleep when Zamel came to bed to lie beside her . . . and hold her.

CHAPTER 10

Even as a new bride, Carrie still worked her movie job six days a week. She Windexed the display cases for packaged candy twice a day, inside and out. She made frequent small batches of popcorn to keep her customers supplied with the freshest. She mopped the space before and after her shift, and greeted returning customers as friends.

At home Carrie made her marriage compatible. She scrubbed the garage, bought curtains for the side door, got storage bins for their clothes and possessions. She got a small stand for the eighteen-inch TV and bought, with her savings, a futon for two. Zamel joined her when he was home in the evenings, sitting next to her. At times he took her hand in his as they watched sitcoms and talent shows, and she felt his usually chilled hand turn warm in hers. At night, he made love to her, exploring her in ways she would relive for days. She kept their sheets clean and washed the blanket twice a week. She learned to cook what he liked from

his cousin's wife, Fatima, who lived in the house next door. On the nights
Zamel never came home and she was alone, she learned to weave mats on
a hand loom Fatima no longer used. Fatima lived in clouds of exhaustion
and suffered from loneliness and shame from having withdrawn from her
wifely duties after her second child was born breech and with difficulties.

Jessie didn't see Carrie at all during this time, and Carrie and Zamel had
no home phone. Jessie missed Carrie's company, and Carrie had never
invited her to Zamel's place. She'd been cut out of Carrie's life. Damn it,
she'd go see her at work. Was Carrie still working? She didn't know, but
it was worth a try. On her afternoon off she went to see *Wonder Woman
II* at the Movieplex. Carrie was behind her counter. Jessie whispered to
her when she thought no one could hear: "I miss you," she confessed.
"What's up with Zamel?"

God, she missed her baby sister talking about her ups and downs;
there had been a loving closeness over the years, especially when Carrie
had moved in and Jessie took on Carrie's troubles as her own.

"He's busy." Carrie smiled. She'd always been chronically content.

"You guys must be rich," Jessie said. "Two jobs and all."

"His mother's in Iran. We send our money to her so she can come
to America."

Carrie gave Jessie a large popcorn without charge. Butter, too.

"Maybe we could hit the mall together sometime?" Jessie asked.

"I can't, Jessie. I've got to be home for Zamel. He comes home at all
hours."

"I'm your sister!"

"Maybe later, after we're settled a little more."

"He'll never love you," Jessie said, then worried she'd sounded too
mean.

Carrie busied herself straightening the candy bar display without a
word.

Jessie held back her anger. Carrie was taking marriage too seriously if
she was turning her back on Jessie, the only family who cared about her
now. And creepy Zamel was obviously a slave master. She doubted this
marriage would last the year. She took her popcorn. Carrie moved away
to start mopping, still smiling. Jessie swore under her breath.

CHAPTER II

A month passed. Jessie heard nothing from Carrie, and amid her persistent loneliness and worry lay a twinge of jealousy that Carrie might be succeeding in her marriage. How could simple Carrie make happiness with a foreign bozo? She had every right to visit Carrie at home; it was, after all, Jessie's obligation to care for her sister. She needed to know what was happening. Was Carrie happy? Who were her friends? Would she and Zamel work out?

Jessie parked her car in front of the two-car garage, set back a few yards from the street. The garage looked flimsy, standing alone on the lot; the only entrance was an undersized door on the side—the two front sliding doors had been nailed immobile with wooden two-by-fours crisscrossing the outside.

The house to the left was nothing but a concrete-block foundation smothered with packed, hardened ashes from a fire years ago. To the right of the garage, the small porch of a one-story house was littered with bicycles and toys and a rusted, ancient barber's chair.

From the back of her car Jessie took out Carrie's rocking chair and approached the garage's side door. Carrie opened it a crack as she approached. Only half of Carrie's face was visible.

"You home alone?" Jessie asked.

Through the narrow opening, only Carrie's pale face was visible. Her frown was stark and unfriendly. "It's a mess in here," Carrie said.

Jessie waited for the door to open, holding the chair for Carrie to see. "I thought you might want this."

Carrie opened the door a little more, then changed her mind and narrowed the opening. "We aren't ready . . ."

"Here. Take the chair," Jessie insisted.

Carrie hesitated, opened the door again, and took the chair.

Jessie strained but could not see her sister's living conditions.

"Some other time, Jessie," Carrie said. "It's too early. Zamel's not dressed."

"I can wait," Jessie said.

"Please don't. Some other time."

Jessie backed away, her curiosity not satisfied. "Okay. Sure," she said, trying to sound lighthearted. "Hey, take care. Call me."

Carrie closed the door without a word.

Jessie strode slowly and deliberately to her car. She slammed her car door, cranked the engine. Zamel yelled to her, running from the garage shirtless, waving his arms, then putting his hands through the armholes of a short-sleeved T-shirt and pulling it on over his head. As he approached, Jessie rolled down the window.

Zamel leaned down to see better. "Miss Jessie. It is kind for you to come. To bring Carrie's chair."

"No problem."

"I wanted to talk."

"You're never quiet, Zamel."

"I might need your help. For my work."

"It's not Christian, but I don't want to help you with your work."

"You don't have to do anything."

"That makes me very happy."

"I must be honest," Zamel said. "I want to see about . . . maybe I could—I mean Carrie and me . . . say, borrow your car sometime. I need for Carrie and me to shop. Maybe for an afternoon?"

"Absolutely not."

"Just for a short time. And maybe I won't need it," he said.

"No."

"Later. Would you maybe shift your mind? For Carrie?"

Jessie rolled up the window. Zamel frowned as she drove off. Jessie could see him in her rearview mirror until she turned the corner at the end of the street and slipped between the trees that lined the two-lane county road.

The night Carrie planned to tell Zamel she was pregnant, he did not come home when expected. They still had no phone at home. Zamel's cell phone was always clipped to his Sansabelt waistband. Carrie checked with Fatima next door, but she had no news.

After eleven, Zamel burst through the door, followed by two dark-skinned men his age. "Go to the back," he said to Carrie.

"Are you all right?" she asked. The tension the three men brought into her home made her afraid.

Zamel did not answer. The men sat on the bed; Zamel pointed Carrie to go outside. Carrie complied, closing the door but standing close, listening to a mix of Arabic and English words: a friend had been arrested, a stolen car had been driven through a glass window into the student center at the college, a bomb had fizzled. She'd heard part of it on the TV news. Even in the silences, she could feel the despair in each of them.

Over the next hour the men's words became earnest and repetitive, with frequent corrections and arguments. When they left, Carrie went in. "Will everything be all right?" she asked.

"Go to bed!" he said.

"I need you tonight."

"I'm spent from my work," he said, taking the only blanket from the bed. "Go to bed!" He sat in the folding chair. "I will sleep here."

She stood still for a moment, wanting to tell him her news. His eyes were closed, his head back, and he was breathing hard and fast. She backed away and went to bed, lying on her back and staring into the dark.

She waited three days to tell him about the baby. They were watching TV on the futon. "I'm pregnant," she said.

He was stunned. "You speak true?"

"We're going to have a baby."

He held her with real joy. "I pray to Allah for a boy," he said.

CHAPTER 12

The Reverend Luther Coffey asked Jessie to dinner. The restaurant table had a red tablecloth, a candle, and silver-plated utensils. He asked about Carrie.

"I'm not sure, but I think she was trying hard to look happy when I saw her," Jessie said.

The Reverend enjoyed Jessie's intensity about everything. And he loved her wholesome look. "A big mistake."

"I told her that!"

"You can't trust foreigners."

"He just wants a woman. Any woman,"."

"Typical," he said. "He sounds as smooth as they come. I've seen a lot of them. Desperate for intimacy. Ready to make their stay in a new country as permanent as they possibly can."

"She wasn't glad to see me the last time. It hurt."

"Is she in danger?"

"Who knows. He's sexist. I imagine they all beat their wives."

"We can't let her heart be broken," he said. "She's too good a person to let that happen."

"I've tried everything!" Jessie said defensively.

"Visit her more often. Even if she turns you away. Try to point out her misery. What it's like in the real world." He wanted Jessie to fill out his empty existence.

"It's useless," she said.

"It's the Christian thing to do," he said. He straightened the silver on each side of his plate, lining it up exactly parallel.

After a silence he thanked God she asked about his family, all but a sister who lived locally. Then he talked about his ministry. The scourge of secularism. Attendance dropping weekly.

After dinner, in the restaurant parking lot, the Reverend opened his car passenger door for Jessie. "Did you have a good time?" he asked.

She didn't answer right away. "I did," she said.

Did he bore her? She did seem to like what he said about Carrie. He was proud to have made firm suggestions. Women liked that. He was pleased she ate dessert. He liked desserts.

On the way to Jessie's apartment, the Reverend pulled into a motel parking lot off the main street and killed the engine.

Jessie looked at him. "What's up?"

"I thought maybe we could spend some time alone together."

"Here?"

"Someplace private. Someplace where the wrong people won't see."

"See what?"

"Us talking together."

"We just went to dinner. We talked at dinner." Jessie frowned. "You want me to go in there?"

"Just for a little while."

"I don't like it. Take me home."

"We could talk here in the car, then. We don't have to get out."

"Instead of going inside a motel?"

He couldn't say what he felt. She seemed unaware of the longing he was suffering.

"I want to go home," she said.

He mustered his courage. "You mean a lot to me, Jessie."

"Not in a motel. Go home. Take a cold shower."

"It's not like that." But it was like that. "We could go somewhere else. I just don't want the congregation gossiping."

She set her jaw and looked away. He started the car, flustered at her refusal. "You've totally misunderstood."

"I'm a better person than you suppose, Reverend."

"You're a good woman, Jessie. I never meant anything else."

She shook her head in disbelief. "A motel! You, of all people."

CHAPTER 13

Patrick—a tall, thin man with an angular face, sharp features, and blue eyes, wearing a white long-sleeved shirt and a rep tie—pulled up his jockey shorts and stepped into a pair of gray slacks. He fastened his genuine alligator belt, turned to a mirrored cabinet over the metal sink, and, taking a comb from his back pocket, slowly, almost tenderly, combed his red hair.

"It's still good, ain't it?" Patrick asked Jessie with pride. It was the energy he delivered during sex that satisfied him. The strength of his hands on the breasts; his gripping of the arms, holding his subject almost in air upon entry. He retrieved his tasseled Italian-leather shoes from under his optometrist's exam chair.

Jessie lay awkwardly on her side on the examining chair, which was reclined to the maximum but still had an angle between the seat and the back.

"You okay?" Patrick asked.

"It hurts," Jessie said. She bent her legs to relieve sharp pains in the vagina.

She slid gingerly off the chair. She was nude except for her panties, which were nestled around her right ankle. She pulled them up and stepped into her pastel-pink uniform pants, finished buttoning her white uniform blouse.

"It didn't hurt last time, did it?" he asked.

"That was different."

"What's wrong?

"This chair hurts me every time," she said. "Sometimes I can't move right for days."

Patrick pulled a paper towel from a wall dispenser and wiped his hands.

"Can't we go somewhere else?" she asked.

Patrick was slipping his arms into his white knee-length professional coat. An ophthalmoscope fell out of the side pocket and clattered to the floor. He swore.

"Did you hear me?" Jessie asked. "This is important."

"Like a motel? You know I can't take the chance now."

"Not a motel. Someplace romantic."

"Not the right time. Too risky."

"When, then?"

"The kids love Christmas. I've got to wait 'till after Christmas."

"You'll tell her about divorce?"

"I promised, didn't I?"

"That was so long ago."

"Here is best. After work. Locked down."

"Could we get a place of our own even before the divorce?"

"Quit complaining, Jessie."

"I'm tired of being convenient on an exam chair that hurts."

"We can do it on the floor. I can shove the slit lamp out of the way."

"That's humiliating."

He was busy pocketing his wallet and his keys, stuffing a few papers and charts into a leather briefcase.

"Do you love me?" Jessie asked.

He shuffled through some charts. "That's hurtful, Jessie. After all this time. How could you ask that?"

"It's not a complicated question. Do you love me? Yes or no?"

"Of course I do. You're everything to me."

"Have you ever hinted you're leaving? Do you talk to her about it?"

He laughed. "God, no. She'd explode."

"Why not tell her now? If you love me?"

Patrick adjusted the exam chair to its normal upright position, ready for tomorrow's first patient. "Stop whining." he said.

"I need respect, Patrick? Just one little pea pod of old-fashioned respect? I'm not a whore off the streets."

Patrick's face reddened. The constant probing irritated him. "I'm tired of this shit."

Jessie's heart pounded. Her mind swirled with accusations mixed with demands for an expression of love. "You're tired? You're tired of making love to me? Is that what you mean?"

"Don't twist my words."

"Say what you mean."

"Stop bitching, Jessie."

"I need to know. I need to know you love me. I can't go on without that."

He latched his briefcase. "You aren't worth this crap."

The sense of her being used broke through, although she knew it had been lurking inside her for months. "I hate you," she said.

He hit her full-face with the flat of his hand. She fell to the floor. He backed away, breathing heavily.

She rose to her knees, groping for the exam chair for support. "Is this the real you?" She felt her face with her fingers.

He hit her again, then stood rigid with anger. Why would this barely competent, impudent assistant turn into a nagging bitch after all he'd given her? Who else would have fucked her? Christ, she looked like the farmer's daughter she was. "You're fired. You've never been any good."

"You're sick," she said.

He refused to speak, trying to get control of himself, trying not to hit her again.

She could not look at him, afraid to confirm that he cared nothing for her. She stood unsteadily, walked to the door, and undid the lock. She walked into the dark office past the reception desk. She grabbed her shoulder bag that had been stuffed out of sight under a counter. She closed the outer door with deliberation and the least amount of sound she could manage.

CHAPTER 14

Dark storm clouds outside made things dimmer than usual in the garage. Carrie arranged her table on an upturned cardboard packing box. She had made two peanut-butter-and-grape-jelly sandwiches on white bread, each on its own paper towel. Sliced wedges of tomato were carefully arranged on a saucer next to a clear glass saltshaker. Two Ball jars were partially filled with orange soda. A single white frosted cupcake, with a red candle stuck in the top, was at one side. She lit the candle with a paper match from a fold-over pack. The flame burned evenly in the still air. Zamel sat cross-legged on the floor. He picked up the sandwich. She sat on the edge of the bed and watched lovingly as he ate.

"Don't stare," he said, "It's rude."

"It's fun being married," she said. "You too?"

Zamel continued eating.

"Well?"

Zamel put down his half-eaten sandwich and salted a tomato slice.

"Say something sweet," she said. "It's our anniversary."

Zamel looked surprised at first but frowned to cover any show of emotion. He ate another tomato slice.

"I know you love me," she said, without a bit of rancor at his aloofness.

Zamel's face remained impassive.

"You're silly," she said. "You are a silly little boy."

Zamel frowned at first at what he took as a rebuke. But when he looked at her he knew she was incapable of intentional hurt. He rendered a faint, contained smile, and his look softened.

"Come on. Say it," she teased.

Zamel laughed. He took her in his arms. He whispered in her ear. "You are the best happening of my entire life."

"Say it, you silly goose."

He laughed and kissed her with growing passion.

"Say you love me!"

He kissed her again, and she knew that he couldn't say those three easy words he thought might diminish him in the world, even though no one would ever know. And it didn't matter.

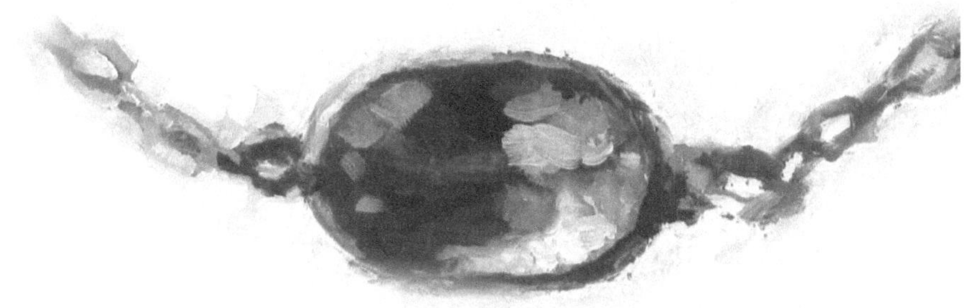

CHAPTER 15

At the Movieplex, Jessie paid for a ticket and passed the ticket taker at the turnstile before she saw Carrie, working alone, filling the roaster pan with popcorn seeds. A few patrons passed by as Jessie walked slowly up to the counter. "Hey, girl," she said.

"Still with butter?" Carrie smiled.

"On a diet. Broke up with Patrick. Got to start looking good."

"He's a jerk," Carrie said.

Carrie handed Jessie a large tub of popcorn. As always, no payment was expected. But Jessie knew Carrie would put money in the till for it after she left.

"I'm looking for work," Jessie said.

Carrie looked radiant. Her skin glowed; her hair was lustrous. She served another customer candy and a Coke. Jessie moved to one side and ate her popcorn until the customer left.

"You guys must be rich. Two jobs and all," Jessie said.

"Zamel's mother is coming from Iran. We send money for her."

"Your place large enough?"

Carrie hesitated, unable to look Jessie in the eye. "I wanted to tell you. We're going to have a baby."

"Oh, no!"

"Zamel wants a boy."

"And you? What do you want?" Jessie asked.

"A boy would be nice. Like Zamel."

"Can you afford it? It costs, like, thousands to have a kid."

"His mama will help."

"His mama will suck up everything you have."

Carrie opened the transparent door of the popper and fluffed the popcorn with a scoop. "We're happy," she said.

"I don't believe that, Carrie. You're living like welfare."

Even in the bustle of the lobby, the silence between them turned awkward. Carrie undid the top button of her shirt, and with the back of her hand showed an almond-size citrine on a silver chain.

Jessie tried to seem unimpressed. "Zamel?" she asked.

"It was his sister's. She died." Carrie buttoned up. She took a paper towel from a roll and wiped the counter intently, although it was already spotless. "You'll miss your show," Carrie said. She turned away from Jessie to another customer and smiled.

Jessie fought off the pain of Carrie's sudden disinterest. She hadn't expected a baby so soon. She should have responded with a little more enthusiasm.

"Call me sometime," Jessie said as she walked away.

Carrie waved, barely looking at her. When Jessie was out of Carrie's sight, she turned toward the exit and dumped her popcorn in a trash can. After a little fuss with the manager, she got a refund for her ticket and left.

CHAPTER 16

Jessie hunted for a job for three weeks before landing a sales job in furniture: a big store all on one level with track lighting and clustered displays. To avoid having to look at herself, she walked around the cheval floor mirror plopped in the center of a bedroom display in a back section of the store. She hated her too-tight pants and white open-necked blouse with plastic buttons on the front and an oval patch above the left breast pocket stitched with "Gripper's Furniture." She had to carry a sign on a short stick that said: "How can I help you?"

She saw Harold Lester enter the store; he walked straight toward her.

"New job?" he asked. He'd shaved off his facial hair and gotten a haircut since she'd seen him, many months ago now, at the museum.

"Go away," she said.

He took out a leather fold-over wallet from his pocket and flashed official identification too fast for her to read it.

"So you're a cop?"

"More like an investigator."

"FBI?"

"I work with them at times."

"And all that BS about old school friends? Church?"

He shrugged. "You like this work?" he asked.

"Temporary. It's barely enough to pay the rent." She positioned her sign in front of Harold. "A dining room suite maybe? I got walnut traditional at 50 percent off."

He shook his head. "I need to ask some questions about this Zamel guy."

"You want a bedroom suite?"

"Come on, Jessie, I'm serious."

"Ms. Broward to you." She wasn't angry, really, just disappointed that he'd lied to her about school. "If he's done something wrong, arrest him. At least that would get him away from my sister."

"There's no proof."

"Of what?"

"Of wrong."

"Is he legal?"

"Still on a student visa."

"Well, he works a lot of jobs."

"You admire him?"

"I don't like him. Too smooth. Sneaky like. But my sister trusts him. They're going to have a baby." Jessie placed her sign on a checkout counter.

"Do you know his friends?" he said.

"My sister doesn't even want me to visit."

"Does she ever mention his friends?"

"I don't talk to her. She doesn't have a phone."

"He has a cell phone."

"I don't think he lets her use it."

"And she's never mentioned his friends. You went there at least once. Talked to her."

"I said ten sentences to her, max, at the house."

"What about the movie place?"

"A few words."

Jessie picked up a sales brochure and handed it to Harold, who did not take it. "Buy a recliner," she said. "Thirty percent off until the end of the week. I get full-price commission on sale items this week only."

"Nothing today."

"You'll be sorry."

"Hard to believe I'll feel sorry about not buying a recliner," he said as he left.

CHAPTER 17

Not knowing about Carrie irritated Jessie. Carrie must be miserable. She probably couldn't escape Zamel's clutches.

She took a sick day off from the furniture store. She parked her car on the street and walked up the drive to Carrie's garage home. She hesitated and then, with a deep sigh, summoned the determination to knock on the door. It opened; Carrie appeared. The dark inside obscured details.

"Hi," Jessie said.

"I didn't know you were coming," Carrie said.

"You don't have a phone. How could I leave a message?"

"Zamel always keeps it with him for business."

"So what am I supposed to do?" Jessie asked. "Not come?"

"It's okay," Carrie said.

Jessie choked up. "It's not been easy, Carrie, without Patrick."

"You miss him?"

"I don't have anyone now." She didn't miss Patrick. It was just that he had left an uncomfortable void in her life.

Carrie opened the door only a few inches. Zamel did not like visitors. But she missed Jessie and her heart filled with pleasure at seeing her. She smiled. "You can meet Zamel's mother."

Mother! Jessie had no idea Mother had arrived. Why had Carrie turned so secretive? She could have sent a note or found a phone to call. Was she ashamed she'd be criticized? Ridiculed? Well, Jessie had only told Carrie the truth, and never tried to persuade her with anything else. Who could fault that? Jessie followed Carrie inside.

Bedsheets were fastened to metal ceiling supports so the garage space was roughly divided in two. Carrie led her past two pallets, each with a blanket folded at the foot but no sheets, that were spread out on the floor about five feet apart. Carrie held a hanging sheet aside for Jessie to enter the other section. There was a double bed and a mattress on a frame, with no headboard. A woman in a dark dress and a *roosari* over her head sat on the floor on a small woven red-and-dark-blue carpet, peeling turnips with a serrated knife.

Jessie leaned over to within a few inches of Mother. She spoke loudly and slowly, moving her lips excessively to exaggerate her diction. "I am Jessie. Do you like America?" she asked.

The woman looked away quickly, smiling insecurely, "Am . air . ka . . . peachy."

"Really," Jessie said. "Nice you came." It sounded meaner than she had meant.

"Mother has nine children," Carrie said.

"Nine?"

Mother kept looking down, *She's pretending the conversation is not about her.*

"When are you due?" Jessie asked Carrie.

"Mother says by the end of next month."

"What does the doctor say?"

Carrie pointed to the bed. "That's where mother sleeps." Carrie took Jessie's hand and led her back through the slit in the hanging sheets. Carrie showed her plastic boxes stacked behind a sheet draped near the door. "I use this for storage."

She pointed to the two pallets. "Zamel and me sleep here while mother is here."

"Looks painful, being pregnant and all and sleeping on the floor."

"Once you get used to it, it's not so bad."

Sad you need to explain away your miserable surroundings, Jessie thought, but she held back a retort.

They went back out to where Mother sat. Carrie directed Jessie a short distance to the sink next to the decades-old four-burner electric stove, with a chipped porcelain oven door. A small knee-high counter refrigerator sat on the floor, a brown extension cord creeping along the wall to an outlet. Carrie opened the refrigerator and handed Jessie a soda.

"Mountain Dew is Mother's favorite," Carrie said. She took a glass from the sink and filled it with tap water.

Jessie grabbed Carrie's arm. "I want to talk to you outside." She muscled Carrie out the door onto the drive. Mother did not look up as they left.

A man rode a mower on the lawn of the house next door. Jessie spoke loudly over the noise. "This is stupid."

"You shouldn't have come," Carrie said.

Jessie handed back the unopened Mountain Dew. "I don't want this."

Carrie put it in her dress pocket, still holding her water glass. The mower was farther away, the noise less loud.

"I am so much happier than I ever was," Carrie said in a normal voice.

"You mean happier without me?" Jessie asked. "With Zamel?"

"It's not about getting away from you."

Jessie tensed, clenching her jaw, her hands in fists. Carrie's initial discomfort at having Jessie there confirmed that she had removed Jessie from her life.

The mower was close again.

"You're living like white trash," Jessie said. "It's embarrassing." She paused intently. "You need a doctor."

"You don't know what I need." But Carrie's face softened as her anger waned; she could never stay angry long. The mower waned, too. "Zamel's a good man," she said. "I'm lucky to have him."

Jessie knew she had overreacted; she felt slightly guilty and more conciliatory. "He's not one of us, Carrie. It's not normal."

Carrie angered again. It wasn't right for Jessie to talk like that. "It's *you* who doesn't belong. Don't come back." The mower noise crescendoed.

"That goddamn mower. Who the hell is that?" Jessie asked.

"George. Zamel's cousin." Carrie said.

"The whole family! How do you stand it?" Jessie shook her head, unable to comprehend.

Carrie wiped tears from her eyes with the back of her hand, then walked back to the garage.

Jessie had failed with Carrie. She had wanted her back, wanted them to be family again.

Jessie walked toward her car. George finished mowing the small patch of grass and drove the mower next to her; he idled the blade.

Jessie was unsure what he intended, but stopped. She saw a woman's face in the window of the house. George shut off the mower. He waved toward the house. "That is Fatima, my wife." Fatima came out of the front door and stood on the step, her hands on her hips. Two children joined her. She spoke to them in an angry tone with foreign words.

"I'm Carrie's sister."

George stared at Jessie. Fatima came out of the house and stood a few feet from them, the children stopped shoulder to shoulder behind her.

"Do you speak English?" Jessie asked George. George was impassive. "You are Zamel's cousin, aren't you?"

"My wife is cousin to the mayor of Hutchings, South Carolina."

La-di-da.

Fatima returned to the house, roughly shoving the children's shoulders to hurry them along; the humid air felt dense with Fatima's hostility.

"Be good to my sister," Jessie said to George.

"She is like family," he said. "We do not want you here."

When Jessie got in her car, George pulled the cord to start the motor. The engine roared.

Jessie's heart was empty. She'd lost Carrie. She would always carry that burden. But worst of all, seeing Carrie, Jessie knew she'd lost the will to be happy. The future held no love or excitement.

CHAPTER 18

I n her final month of pregnancy, Carrie washed dishes by hand standing at the sink in the garage apartment. Zamel's mother sat away from Carrie on the bed with a plastic container on her knees, snapping beans. Carrie jerked with surprise and an instant of fear when Zamel and his two stranger comrades, Habib and Tahmin, entered through the side door of the garage. Zamel's mother continued with her work, unperturbed.

The distress on Zamel's face pained Carrie's heart. "What's happened?"

"Nothing. Go to the back."

"Tell me what's wrong."

"Be quiet. Take Mother."

The two women went behind the hanging sheets that separated the two areas. Tahmin sat on the bed; Habib squatted on the floor. Zamel pulled up the only chair to a folding card table and sat. They said nothing for more than a minute, Habib breathing deeply. Tahmin placed a laptop computer on the table. "See if it works," he said. Zamel plugged in the power cord after taking the TV plug out of the wall socket. The computer screen lit after a few seconds.

Zamel laughed humorously. "It turns on."

"Does it have enough whatever?"

Zamel navigated for a few seconds. "Not enough memory. And the software is not here. I will look in all the files. But I don't think it's there."

"How could I know?" Habib said defensively.

"Is it his computer? You're sure?" Tahmin asked Habib.

"It was on his desk, in a briefcase. Why wouldn't it be his?" Habib answered.

Tahmin swore. "Look again," he said to Zamel.

"I cannot test it thoroughly now," Zamel said. "Take hours."

"You will have to go back to find another," Tahmin said to Habib.

Habib shrugged. "Let him see if it works," he said, nodding to Zamel.

"He cannot raise suspicion where he works," Tahmin said.

Carrie stuck her head between the sheets. Her face was intent with concern and curiosity. "Do you want something to drink?" she asked.

"Leave us," Zamel said sharply.

Habib stood and walked to Carrie. He briefly touched her cheek with the back of his hand. He grinned. "You are woman for gods."

"Don't touch her," Zamel said. Habib backed away.

"We have things to do," Tahmin said.

Habib gave a short, cruel laugh as Carrie retreated behind the sheets.

Zamel glanced to the computer. "I will test it tonight." Tahmin and Habib moved to the door.

"You must never come here again," Zamel said.

"We will come when we need to," Habib said. Zamel stayed motionless until they were gone.

Carrie rushed out from behind the sheets. Mother stayed seated and could be seen as a shadow through the sheet barrier. "Tell me, Zamel," Carrie begged.

"You must never know. Even I do not know the details."

In despair at being excluded Carrie went behind the screen and leaned against the wall. It was the first time she'd felt this way with Zamel.

Zamel's mother sat on a pallet and continued with her beans; the snaps were loud now. Mother purposely did not look at Carrie. Carrie suspected that Mother knew more than she let on, but since Mother did not talk to her in any language, there was no way to be sure.

CHAPTER 19

Weeks later, Jessie sat at same table in the mall that she and Carrie had sat at while waiting for Zamel more than a year before. The food court was busy but not crowded. She had a large cup of black coffee in front of her and a paper boat containing a few remaining French fries. She'd come to shop, maybe see someone she knew.

She stared vacantly toward the escalators. Harold Lester emerged and walked toward her. She hadn't seen him since he had come to the furniture store. She looked away to discourage him.

"Fries kill you," he said.

"You a doctor?"

"I care about your health."

"You care about my brother-in-law?"

He pulled out a chair and sat down.

"Please don't sit there," Jessie said. She tried to appear offended, but she was curious. Why was he still following her?

"Why so hostile?" Harold asked, sitting down.

Jessie shrugged. "I don't like all this sneaky stuff."

"I could take you out to dinner." He smiled.

Ridiculous. She wished there was a rock to hide under.

"Would that be okay?" he asked. "Dinner?"

"No. Why are you here?"

"I would never talk business at dinner with you," he said.

"You got enough to grab him yet?"

"No."

Harold leaned back and stretched out his legs. "You went out to your sister's again. What did she say?"

"She said very specifically, 'Don't talk to bald old men with mustaches.'"

"She give a reason?"

"They're jerks."

"Anything else?"

"And serious health risks."

"Nothing new about Zamel?"

"Not one thought to report. He wasn't there." Jessie saw a security guard near the elevator. "I don't like you stalking me," she said, waving to the guard for help. She'd file a complaint.

Harold turned so the guard could see him, and held up his hand in a friendly greeting. The guard stopped and smiled. Harold gave a thumbs up. The guard walked in the opposite direction.

"What did all that mean?" Jessie said.

"I'm not a threat." Harold said.

"Then why do you keep coming around unannounced?"

He smiled. "Sometimes you're more likable than you want to be."

"I'll bet I'm a lot less likable than you think I am." Jessie stood, picking up her bag. "What's Zamel done wrong?"

"Nothing I know of exactly. He's suspected."

"Immigration?"

"Can't say."

"A terrorist?"

"I can't prove it."

"Then why are you here?"

"It's my job."

"You're creepy." Jessie rose quickly, grabbed her shoulder bag, and walked away.

Harold caught up. He handed her a card. "Call me if you need me. If you think of anything important."

"I think I'll tell Zamel about you."

He smiled. "You think I would talk about him if he didn't know?"

"Well, I'll tell him anyway? To scare him away from my sister. Maybe she could grow up normal." She walked away, not sure where she was going, but making an effort to appear purposeful.

She did not know what Harold did, really. Internal security? Police? FBI? Her best guess was that he worked as an immigration official. She doubted Zamel was still legally in the country.

Jessie called the number on the card Harold gave her, hoping to find out who he worked for. But it went directly to him and she hung up when he answered.

CHAPTER 20

The same evening, Jessie went up the stairs to her apartment and found Carrie sitting on the floor leaning against her apartment door, her infant wrapped in a blanket in her arms. When she saw Jessie, Carrie stopped nursing and discreetly buttoned her shirt.

Jessie knelt to see the baby better. "What's up? You okay?" Jessie pulled back the blanket. She still did not approve of mixed-marriage offspring, but she was drawn in by the fragile beauty of this newborn. The baby burped. "You want to come in?" Jessie asked.

"Is it all right?" Carrie asked tentatively.

"You're not planning to move in, are you?" The hurt on Carrie's face made Jessie regret her remark.

Carrie sat on the two-seater sofa and laid the baby beside her, moving a pillow to prevent it from sliding off.

"Zamel kick you out?" Jessie asked.

"That's so mean," Carrie said.

"Well, tell me."

"He takes good care of me, Jessie."

"And his mother? She taking good care of you, too?"

"She may be going back to Iran . . . I think so . . . her visa's up. But she needs money. Zamel's taken on another job. He's never home."

"How do you put up with it?"

"He loves me."

"He can't love you."

"Doctor Patrick didn't love you."

"That's different."

"Zamel cares."

Jessie couldn't hide her irritation, and Carrie's reference to Patrick shamed her when she thought how she had succumbed to his lust, in the clutch of sin. Carrie was right, there had been no love with Patrick like Carrie seemed to have with Zamel. Jessie felt a pang of jealousy.

"Zamel will leave," Jessie said. "You'll be alone with the baby."

"He will not. He's trying to get his green card."

Now Jessie wanted to hurt. "Did you know there's an investigator following him? He's been asking me questions about Zamel for months. He's got government identification. He won't say exactly, but I think he's immigration." She looked away and paused before she met Carrie's gaze again. "Is Zamel a terrorist?"

"He's not a terrorist!" Carrie said. But Jessie heard the hesitancy of doubt in Carrie's voice. Carrie might suspect, too.

"Something's happened," Jessie said.

"Has not."

"He bring you here?"

"I took the bus."

"When's the last time you saw him?" Jessie asked.

"A week."

"You really did hope to move in here, didn't you?"

"I just wanted to see you." Carrie looked away suddenly, her face tense and anxious with exhaustion.

The awkward silence isolated each in her own world. The baby gave a little cry. Carrie rocked the child gently.

"Is it Zamel's mother?" Jessie asked.

"She loves Golshan, Jessie."

"Does she speak English yet?"

"She doesn't try. She won't turn on the TV to learn."

"Does she talk to you?"

Carrie adjusted the baby in her arms. She sobbed. "I'm so lonely."

Jessie sat beside Carrie on the sofa. Touched her hand.

Carrie cried as she touched the baby's mouth with her finger. "Oh, Jessie, he can't tell me things. And I get so lonely when he's gone."

"What about his cousin next door? His wife? They talk to you?"

"She doesn't like me anymore. He won't speak to me now."

Jessie leaned back on the sofa and put her head back. "I don't have enough room here for the two of you."

"I could never leave Zamel," Carrie said.

"He's left you, without a word."

"He always comes back. He needs me, Jessie. He's not a strong man sometimes." Jessie paused with her eyes closed. "But he's stubborn. He doesn't believe in himself sometimes. But he's kind to me."

"He's out for himself, Carrie. Anyone can see that."

They sat in silence for many minutes, Carrie rocking the baby now. Carrie touched Jessie's arm. "It's too late to go back," Carrie said. "Could we at least stay tonight?"

Jessie pulled the blanket to one side to look at the baby. She touched her index finger to a little hand that clamped down, a tiny but strong grasp that sparked a wave of emotions—attraction, caring, and a deep sadness. Jessie, with her gaze, let Carrie know they could stay the night. She held back on mentioning that she wanted them back with her to stay as long as they wanted.

Jessie brought in blankets and pillows to fashion a makeshift crib. Carrie lay on the sofa, her head back, her eyes closed . . . but not asleep. Her hand protected the baby beside her. The baby whimpered. Carrie stood and cradled the baby in her arms. "Hold her," she said to Jessie. Jessie took the baby. Carrie went into the bathroom and shut the door.

The baby whimpered again and started to cry. Jessie, her face impassive, tightened her grip on the child and swung from side to side. The child stopped crying, the face relaxed.

The baby soon slept, her face toward Jessie. The child's beauty was unique; she had the fine features and glowing skin of a Persian princess. Jessie felt an unchecked love for the child, and its unexpected intensity made her uncomfortable.

Carrie returned and reached for the baby. For an instant Jessie did not to want to let go.

"What is her name again?" Jessie asked.

"Golshan."

After Carrie and Golshan were settled, Jessie went to the kitchenette to prepare something to eat. Three hard knocks on the door startled her. Golshan cried. Jessie went to the door, silently tiptoeing on the carpet. She was breathing hard. She touched nothing but placed her ear against the panel. Someone beat a fist against the door again, five times. She pulled back.

"Zamel?" Carrie called from the couch. Silence. Both women listened.

"Who is it?" Jessie finally asked.

"It's me," the voice said.

"It's Zamel," Carrie said. Jessie opened the door.

Zamel pushed his way in. "Get your belongings, wife."

"Calm down," Jessie said. Carrie would not move.

Zamel stuffed baby things into Carrie's tote bag and grabbed her arm, pulling her up. "Get Golshan."

Jessie faced Zamel. "Leave them alone." She feared for Carrie now, and for Golshan.

"It's okay, Jessie," Carrie said, standing and wrapping Golshan in a blanket.

Zamel shoved Carrie and the baby out the door and followed, carrying the bag.

"You left her. You creep," Jessie said.

"Jessie, I warn you, do not interfere." His eyes were hard with anger.

Jessie stood in the apartment doorway as they disappeared down the stairs at the end of the hall.

Zamel said nothing in the borrowed truck he took Carrie and Golshan home in.

"I was just lonely," Carrie said, but Zamel did not reply. When they entered the garage apartment, Mother took Golshan. Zamel took Carrie's hand and led her behind the hanging sheets where he made tender love to her and held her until she slept, the first peaceful sleep she'd had in months.

CHAPTER 21

After the breakup with Patrick, and each day dreading to go to the furniture store, Jessie started going regularly to church again. She'd heard nothing from Carrie or Zamel. She was afraid a visit to the garage might draw attention from Harold Lester.

Sunday-morning sunrays pierced the branches of the oaks in the church yard, blanketing the front of the building and its steeple with variegated shadows patched with intense reflections from the white paint. The Reverend Luther Coffey, his back to the sun, greeted parishioners as they left the service. "Thank you so much for coming," he said with fragile sincerity to an elderly woman. "I'm so glad you're feeling better."

Jessie bypassed the line and circled away from the Reverend. He excused himself from the next in line and walked quickly to her, touching her arm to make her stop. "Could we talk?"

"There is nothing to talk about."

"About Carrie."

How could Jessie know his true motives? The lech. Should she agree or leave? After all, he had wanted to take her to a motel! But she'd come to believe he was too inexperienced with women to want more than talk.

"Please," he said. "I will be only a minute."

Jessie waited at the edge of the walkway that led from the church. Her Sunday-go-to-meeting low-heeled shoes hurt her feet. She wanted to be home, to kick them off.

In a few minutes, the Reverend approached her and pointed to a bench on the church lawn. "We could sit over there," he said.

When they sat, Jessie kept a respectable distance between them.

"I haven't seen Carrie in church," the Reverend said. "Has she lost faith?"

"She doesn't have a car. Butner is a long way without a car."

"Could you bring her to church sometime?"

"Look, I don't run her life. She does what she wants."

Jessie started to stand but the Reverend prevented her with his hand. "It's her husband, Zamel. He wants to convert."

Jessie shook her head in disbelief. "It can't be true."

"He paid the fee," the Reverend said. "He asked me questions about commitment. Baptism. Where we go in the hereafter. He bought a Bible. It's like a miracle."

"You can't believe him."

"He paid the fee."

"And you took the fee? From him? I never thought you'd charge him, or anyone, for joining the church."

"I didn't know what to do. He seemed so sincere. I didn't want him to mistrust me."

"It was wrong. He'll mistrust you anyway when he finds out. The church never charges for admission." She was aware she was defending Zamel and it surprised her.

The Reverend looked away. "I'll refund it when he gets started. That will be the right thing to do." He thought for a few seconds. "Maybe you could talk to Carrie. Convince her to start coming to church with Zamel."

"Why don't you visit Carrie?"

"We could go together."

Jessie laughed. "I don't think so."

"Why not?"

"It should be a church call."

The Reverend squinted slightly. "You two not getting along?"

"You go. Make the church seem to want her."

The Reverend reached for her hand but she drew away. "I could do that with you," he said earnestly.

"It's not right. Mixing God's business by taking me with you."

"You're her sister. It's not a date."

"Who can tell with you?"

The pain of her remark showed on his face. "That's unfair," he said, with a touch of contrition. Jessie stood.

"Can I call you next week?" he asked.

She hesitated. He was sincere. Now she was convinced the motel incident was definitely a misguided mistake by an inexperienced man.

"I would prefer not," she said.

CHAPTER 22

Jessie couldn't stop thinking about Zamel's new commitment to the church. She didn't believe he would follow through and was suspicious that the money he paid was stolen or counterfeit. She took a sick day off from the furniture store and went to see Carrie at home.

Carrie sat outside the garage, her back against the garage door, her knees up, nursing Golshan. Jessie parked; as she approached, Carrie kept her head down and Jessie squatted to see her face. Carrie was crying.

"What's up?" Jessie asked.

Carrie finished nursing and buttoned her shirt.

"Look at me!" Jessie insisted.

Carrie's eyes were frightened. She seemed trapped in indecision, the way Jessie remembered seeing her in their youth. Carrie could not take control of her life when she was this anxious. She retreated into herself, frozen in thought like a frightened rabbit in a bright headlight.

"Come with me," Jessie said.

"Golshan. I can't."

"Bring her."

"I'll leave her with Mother."

"Bring her."

Carrie finally followed Jessie. They sat in the car. Golshan slept peacefully.

"I'm taking you home," Jessie said. "Enough of this."

"I don't want that," Carrie said.

"What's wrong?"

Carrie cried for a minute or more before she could find words. "Mother's going back to Iran. I think she wants to take Golshan with her. Her 'sweet grandchild.'"

"She's told you this?"

"No. She still speaks only a few words I can understand. Zamel told me."

"How do you know she's leaving?"

"She has long talks with Zamel's cousin's wife next door. Mother takes Golshan with her. When I am at work, Golshan stays there like family."

"What does Zamel say?"

"He says his mother would never take Golshan away."

"And you believe him?"

"I don't know. I don't think he sees what I see," Carrie said.

"Do you think he wants Golshan to grow up in Iran?"

Carrie hesitated. "I don't think so."

"Did you ask him?"

Carrie didn't speak.

Jessie started the car. "I'm taking you away."

Carrie opened the door. "No. I cannot leave Zamel." She had her feet on the ground.

Jessie cut the motor. "That's crazy. Get back in," she said. "Let me hold Golshan."

Carrie handed Golshan to Jessie and settled again in the seat, closing the door. Jessie felt the warmth of the child on her breast. She pressed her cheek against Golshan's head, felt the infinite softness of the black hair. "Zamel's in trouble, Carrie. The authorities have contacted me again, asking questions."

Carrie sobbed.

"What do you really know about Zamel?" Jessie asked.

Carrie did not respond for a minute. "He wouldn't do anything wrong."

"You don't believe that."

"He is not a bad person," Carrie said. "I know that."

"Would you know if he was in deep trouble?"

Carrie looked away as if threatened by the question.

"You can't let it hurt Golshan," Jessie said.

Carrie faced the truth. Her face hardened. Then she took Golshan from Jessie. She opened the car door and walked back to the garage without looking back.

Carrie loved Zamel. It was obvious. Jessie would pray that Carrie's loyalty and caring and unwavering decency would not destroy her life— and Golshan's.

Harold Lester approached a uniformed Jessie in the furniture store, standing near a canopy bed with her sign. For the first time she was relieved to see him.

"Have you heard from Zamel?" he asked. "You went out to see your sister."

"We didn't discuss Zamel," she said.

"Come on. Did she tell you he hasn't been home in more than a week, and he hasn't been to his job in three days?"

Jessie didn't look at him.

"Something's going on, Jessie. We need to know what it is."

"He's joining the church."

"Really?"

"He's taking classes to convert."

"Anything else?"

"What else do you expect?"

"Anything that would tell us where he is and what he's up to."

"My sister thinks he is not bad. That he would do nothing wrong."

Harold laughed. "And she'd be the last to know, wouldn't she?"

"He loves her," Jessie said. "I'm sure of that."

"Do you think that's enough to divert wrongdoing?"

"I don't know. I hope so."

Harold looked serious. "He was trained in Afghanistan, Jessie.

Explosives. Computers. That's a lot of dedication. It can't all be innocent."

Carrie can't be wrong about Zamel. "Go away," she said.

"Think about that dinner, sometime," Harold said.

Jessie shook her head and left before Harold could say anything more.

Jessie awoke to a pounding on the front door, slipped on her slippers, and felt her way in her nightgown into the living room in the semi-darkness.

"Who is it?"

"I have a message," a voice said.

"Who are you?" Jessie whispered.

"A friend of Zamel."

The voice did not sound threatening, but still Jessie was afraid. "Please open," the voice said. "It is urgent."

"Tell me."

"I cannot speak it through the door."

Jessie undid the bolt and chain. A small dark youth wearing a hoodie slipped in. "It is Zamel. He must talk to you. He cannot come here. You are being watched. I am to write instructions for you so that you will not be followed."

"Where are Carrie and Golshan?" Jessie asked.

"His wife is with him."

"His daughter, too?"

"I do not know."

Jessie gave him a pencil and notepaper. Sitting at the kitchen table, the youth detailed how to find Zamel and Carrie.

Jessie dressed, went to her car, drove four blocks, then pulled into a side street, turned off the motor and lights and waited, searching for anyone who might be following. After fifteen minutes only two cars passed. She started driving again. She followed directions for a circuitous route into Raleigh, to a multistory public parking garage. She found a spot on the fourth level, then took the elevator to the fifth level and waited near the stair exit. In minutes, Zamel emerged from the shadows.

She followed him out of the garage, onto a side street. He walked more than a quarter of a mile to an all-night diner. He motioned for her to go down the alley at the side of the diner while he watched the street.

Behind the building, hidden by a dumpster, Carrie huddled, cradling Golshan in her arms. Carrie cried out with joy when she saw Jessie. Jessie kissed her and sat down, pulling the edge of the blanket back to see if Golshan was really there. Zamel joined them and squatted, his body tense, his eyes searching the darkness nervously.

"We are leaving," Zamel said. "Carrie wanted to see you. To say goodbye."

"Where are you going?"

"I cannot say. We will start a new life."

"In Iran?"

"Not Iran."

"To do more bad things?"

"No. Nothing bad. To make a good life."

"We don't want to be away from you, Jessie," Carrie said.

"This is true," Zamel said. "But we must go."

"The authorities will follow," Jessie said. "They know all about you."

"They are not the only ones we abandon now. Men I've worked with will not approve of our leaving."

"Who?"

"Ones who are more capable of finding us than the authorities."

Jessie looked to Carrie. "Are you in danger?"

Carrie looked away and stood as Zamel rose. "We've got to keep moving," Carrie said.

"I have friend who can help," Zamel said. "We will go there and he will help us find somewhere safe."

"How? Do you have a car?"

"We will find a way."

"Where is it?"

"It is many miles," Zamel said.

"We can do it, Jessie," Carrie said.

"I have money," Zamel said, "but we must avoid the public authorities. They will be looking."

"And you don't know how you will get there," Jessie said. She could not take her eyes off Golshan.

Neither Carrie nor Zamel spoke as they prepared to leave. Golshan slept peacefully, unaware of her parents' urgency and stress.

Jessie's love for all three of them flooded through her. Her heart ached. "I will take you wherever you need to go."

Carrie and Zamel stared at her with surprise. Neither had been prepared to ask, and neither had ever expected her to offer. They'd come to say goodbye.

Jessie took control. "I'll get the car. Tell me where it's safe to pick you up."

Five hours later Jessie said goodbye to them in a residential neighborhood in the suburbs of Washington, DC. She did not know where they would go from there. She hugged Carrie and kissed Golshan. She turned to embrace Zamel but, embarrassed, he backed away. Jessie moved closer and took Zamel in her arms. "Take good care of them, Zamel. I love you all."

Zamel embraced her and put his head on her chest, his head under her chin.

"We love you . . ." Carrie said.

Zamel held Jessie's hand. "I am forever grateful . . ."

"Don't," Jessie said.

"But you have been . . ."

"You're family, Zamel." She grasped his shoulders.

And they were gone.

Jessie drove back to her apartment and called in sick the next morning. Harold Lester knocked on her door not much later.

"Where is he, Jessie? Something's about to go down. I need to know."

"I don't know," she said, keeping the door opening narrow so he would not come in.

"You got past us last night. We know you bought gas in Virginia with a credit card."

"He's innocent."

"That's not a judgment you can make."

"I can and I will."

"Where did you take them?"

"He's not evil. He's husband to my sister and father of my niece."

"And you shouldn't have any hesitation about telling us where he is."

Jessie sighed. "I don't know and there is no way I can find out."
"I can't believe that."
"Believe what you want. I would never betray them."
"That could be obstruction—"
Jessie closed the door, sliding the dead bolt in place.

CHAPTER 23

Jessie was fired from the furniture store for lack of enthusiasm and took a secretarial job at the Reverend Coffey's church. A year and seven months later they were married, and a few weeks after that the Reverend accepted a church position in Wilmington.

Jessie had never heard or expected a word from Carrie and Zamel. But one morning, at their modest bungalow near the beach, she walked to the mailbox before leaving for work. She flipped through the letters to find a manila envelope with no return address, forwarded from Atlanta. The handwriting was not familiar. The smudged postmark was unreadable. Inside she found a color photo of a four-year-old girl on her way up the walk to a century-old house with a wraparound porch and a hanging sign that said "Betty Potter's Pre-Kindergarten." The girl wore a white dress trimmed in lace that covered her dark legs to just above the knee, white socks, and white Mary Janes. She carried a shiny black plastic book bag that looked empty. She was grinning at the camera, her brown eyes gleaming with excitement and confidence. A woman was coming down the walk from the house toward her, her arms out, welcoming.

A sticky note said, "First day. Love you."

"Honey," Jessie yelled toward the house.

The Reverend Coffey emerged in a T-shirt and drawstring pajama bottoms holding a diapered infant in his arms.

"Look," Jessie said, holding up the photo, her eyes moist. "They're okay."

Books by William H. Coles

McDowell
Creating Literary Stories: A Guide for Fiction Writers
Illustrated Short Fiction of William H. Coles 2000-2016
Short Fiction of William H. Coles 2000-2016
The Surgeon's Wife
The Spirit of Want
Sister Carrie
Facing Grace with Gloria and Other Stories
The Necklace and Other Stories
Story in Literary Fiction: A Manual for Writers
Literary Fiction as an Art Form: A Text for Writers
The Short Fiction of William H. Coles 2001-2011
The Illustrated Fiction of William H. Coles 2000-2012

storyinliteraryfiction.com

Short Stories by William H. Coles

The Gift, Speaking of the Dead, Homunculus,
Suchin's Escape, The Wreck of the Amtrak's Silver Service,
The Indelible Myth, The Stonecutter, The Necklace,
Nemesis, The Bear, Gatemouth Willie Brown on Guitar,
The Golden Flute, Dilemma, The Amish Girl,
Dr Greiner's Day in Court, The Cart Boy, Lost Papers,
Inside the Matryoshka, Big Gene, Grief,
The Miracle of Madame Villard, Clouds, Reddog,
The War of the Flies, Crossing Over, Father Ryan,
Facing Grace with Gloria, The Perennial Student,
The Activist, Curse of a Lonely Heart,
On the Road to Yazoo City, Captain Withers's Wife,
The Thirteen Nudes of Ernest Goings

Available on <u>storyinliteraryfiction.com</u>